19 20 21 22 23 24 25 26 27 28 29 30 31 32 33 34 35 36 37 38 39 40 41 42 43 44 45 46 47 48 49 50 51 52 53 54 55 56 57 58 59 60 61 62 63 64 65 66 67 68 69 70 71 72 73 74 75 76 77 78 79 80 81 82 83 84 85 86 87 88 89 90 91 92 93 94 95 96 97 98 99 100

1 2 3 4 5 6 7 8 9 10 11 12 13 14 15 16 17 18

 For Bluebell

Henry Holt and Company, LLC
*Publishers since 1866*
115 West 18th Street
New York, New York 10011
www.henryholt.com

Henry Holt is a registered trademark of Henry Holt and Company, LLC
Copyright © 2002 by Tony Ross
All rights reserved.
First published in the United States in 2003 by Henry Holt and Company
Distributed in Canada by H. B. Fenn and Company Ltd.
Originally published in the United Kingdom in 2002 under the title *One Hundred Shoes* by Andersen Press Ltd.

Library of Congress Cataloging-in-Publication Data
Ross, Tony.
Centipede's 100 shoes / by Tony Ross.
Summary: A little centipede buys shoes to protect his feet but finds that
they are a lot of trouble to put on and take off.
[1. Centipedes—Fiction. 2. Shoes—Fiction.]   I. Title.
PZ7.R71992On 2003     [E]—dc21          2002012841

ISBN 0-8050-7298-5
First American Edition—2003

Printed in Italy

3  5  7  9  10  8  6  4

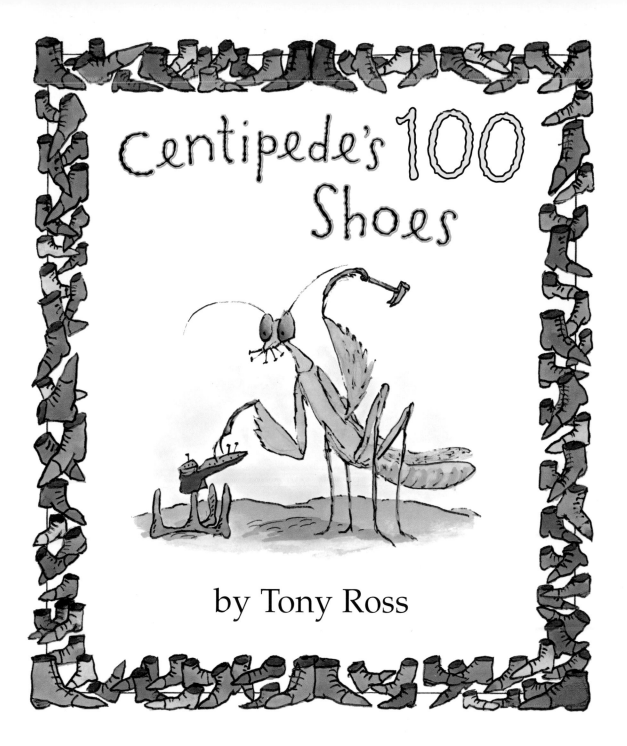

# Centipede's 100 Shoes

## by Tony Ross

Henry Holt and Company

New York

"Ow!"

The little centipede was not looking where he was going, and he hurt his toe.

But which one? Not this one, or this one . . .
"Mom will know!"

"I'll kiss it better," said Mom. "Is it this one, or this one, or this one, or this one, or this one, or this one . . . ?"

At last, Mom found the hurt toe and kissed it better.
"Tomorrow you must get some shoes," she said.

Early the next morning, the little centipede's mom took him to the shoe store.

"One hundred shoes, please!" said the little centipede.
"Fifty left ones, and fifty right ones."

"Why do you want one hundred?" asked the shoe seller.
"Because I'm a centipede, which means a hundred feet,"
said the little centipede.

"Do you want lace-ups or buckles?" asked the shoe seller.
"Lace-ups, please," said the little centipede. "Lace-ups are more grown-up."

So the little centipede tried on shoes until he found ones
that he liked, and the shoe salesman wrapped them up.

The next day, the little centipede put on his shoes. It took a long time. Then he had to tie up all the laces, and when at last he had finished . . .

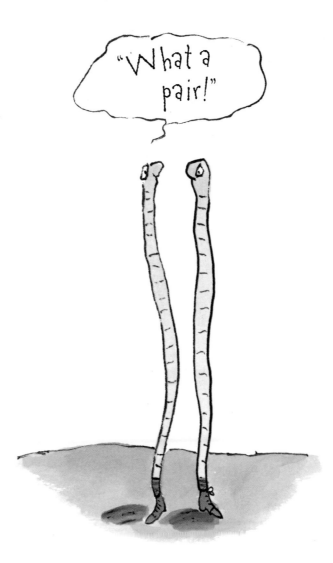

. . . for two worms.

. . . with socks for the five spiders,
and with enough shoes and socks left . . .

. . . and gave them all to friends with fewer legs.

He gave shoes to five spiders, four beetles, two woodlice, and a grasshopper . . .

So he put his one hundred shoes and his forty-two socks
into his little wheelbarrow . . .

The next morning, the little centipede looked at all the shoes and socks.

"Oh, I don't think I'll bother!" he sighed.

So the little centipede took off his shoes and tumbled into bed. "You can't go to sleep in your socks!" said his mother. So he took off his socks as well.

Right after supper, he went for a walk.
"My feet feel fine now, Mom," he said.
"Time for bed," said his mother.

The next morning, the little centipede put on all his socks.
He had his lunch, then started to put on his shoes.

. . . and his aunties all began to knit socks.

"That's because you have no socks on," said his mother.
And the little centipede started to take off his shoes again . . .

So after lunch, he went for a walk.
"Oh, Mom!" he cried. "My new shoes hurt!"

The next morning, the little centipede put on his shoes again.
This time he was quicker, and he was better at tying the laces.

And then it was bedtime, and time to start taking the
shoes off again.

. . . he had fifty-eight shoes left over.

"That's because most centipedes have only forty-two legs," said his granddad.